Spirit Brides

BOOKS BY KAHLIL GIBRAN IN THIS SERIES

Spirit Brides

BY

KAHLIL GIBRAN

TRANSLATED BY JUAN R. I. COLE

WHITE CLOUD PRESS
SANTA CRUZ, CA

FIRST EDITION

Cover Illustration by Kahlil Gibran, Gift of Mrs. Mary Haskell Minis
Courtesy, Museum of Fine Arts, Boston
Cover Design by Daniel Cook
Printed in the United States of America

Library of Congress Cataloging in Publication Data
Gibran, Kahlil, 1883-1931
    ['Ará'is al-murúj. English]
    Spirit Brides / by Kahlil Gibran; translated by Juan R. I. Cole.
    p.   cm.
    ISBN 1-883991-00-5 : $16.00
    I. Cole, Juan Ricardo. II. Title
PJ7826.I2A913   1993
892'.735--dc20   93-29515
                                        CIP

Illustration credits
All illustrations by Kahlil Gibran
Untitled oil, p. 2; Portrait of the Artist's Mother, p. 8; Crossed Open Embrace, p. 22; Artist's sister, p. 24; Heavenly Mother, p. 31; Head of Orpheus Floating Down the River Hebrus to the Sea, p. 46; Self portrait, back cover, Gifts of Mrs. Mary Haskell Minis, in the collection of Telfair Academy of Arts and Sciences, Savannah, Georgia. Nude figures pointing, page 70, Gift of Mrs. Mary Haskell Minis, Courtesy of Museum of Fine Arts, Boston.

CONTENTS

Translator's Acknowledgments

I wish first of all to thank the many Lebanese friends I made in Beirut during the 1970s, who collectively gave me invaluable insights into their culture and language. They did so selflessly and graciously, despite the tribulations that were befalling them during the opening years of the Civil War. In 1978-1979 while in Beirut, I translated late-breaking Arabic news stories into English for the Monday Morning Company, often by candlelight because artillery duels had temporarily knocked out the electricity; I owe a special debt of gratitude to my editor and colleagues there. Without that Lebanese experience, producing this rendering would have been much more difficult.

My wife, Shahin, has been endlessly supportive and is the source of many perceptive comments on this text, which immeasurably improved it. My editor and publisher at White Cloud, Steven Scholl, has shown unwavering faith in and enthusiasm for this project. Brian Miller made many valuable suggestions, from which this translation benefited. My dear friend and colleague John Walbridge, fellow Gibran scholar and translator, has been a constant source of encouragement and ideas.

Introduction

Kahlil Gibran's *The Prophet* has attracted readers in enormous numbers ever since its publication in 1923, so that he is said to be the bestselling American poet of all time, albeit he most often wrote prose poetry rather than verse as such. His prose poems owe much to the influence on him of American writers such as Walt Whitman. Gibran did not begin his career by writing in English, nor by producing philosophical essays alone. Rather, among his first published works were two innovative collections of short stories that came out in 1906 and 1908 (*Spirit Brides* and *Rebellious Spirits*) and a novel (*Broken*

Wings) that appeared in 1912. These books, written when he was in his twenties, are characterized by a lyrical and dynamic style far different from the stolid classicism that had dominated Middle Eastern literature up until that time.

The U.S. readers of the 1920s and 1930s who made *The Prophet* such a success would have been surprised to hear of the existence of these earlier works, since they were penned in Arabic and published at an expatriate press in New York City. The period between 1880 and 1924 was (like the era since 1965) a time of greatly increased immigration to the United States; during those decades many immigrants came for the first time from the Eastern Mediterranean, from Sicily and Greece and Eastern Europe and Mount Lebanon, in short, from the Austro-Hungarian, Russian and Ottoman Empires. Kahlil's family, who arrived in the U.S. virtually penniless in 1895, was typical of this wave of immigration.

Although Gibran's artistic talent was quickly spotted by social workers in Boston when he was only twelve years old, and he gained the patronage thereafter of Boston notables such as Fred Holland Day and Mary Haskell, the immigrant network of young Lebanese-Americans around him remained a prime social reference. It was for them that he wrote his prose poems and vignettes for Arabic journals, which were later collected in such books as *A Tear and a Smile* and *The Storms*, and for them that he produced literary works such as *Spirit Brides* (literally the title might be rendered "Brides of the Meadows," a reference to a Lebanese folk belief in vengeful naiads). It was not until 1948 that *Spirit Brides* was first translated into English, with an unfortunate title. The existing English translations have been called by one Gibran scholar "free and largely inaccurate." Even were this not the case, decades have elapsed since they were carried out, and our language and literary sensibilities have changed so much that new translations are called for. The present version seeks to be the first academically sound rendering of a major Gibran work.

American readers who have enjoyed *The Prophet* will be keenly interested in Gibran's earlier literary works both because they stand as eminently readable and because they show the development of Gibran's thought. Here, he expresses forthright anger and outrage about social injustice, combined with a steadfast faith in the perseverance of the human spirit, all in a style that is graceful, fresh, and natural. These narratives, which appeared during the same era that produced the social criticism of Jack London and Upton Sinclair, differ greatly from the sober and oracular works Gibran authored in English two decades later.

On the other hand, many of the themes in *The Prophet* are foreshadowed in the early stories. The first piece here, "The Ash of Centuries and the Immortal Flame," is about a love that survived death and the destruction of the ancient Phoenician civilization in which it flourished. The anguish of love, endured by Nathan when his beloved abruptly dies as a result of the jealousy of the spirit brides of the valley, presages the reminder by Almustafa of Orphalese that love is a scimitar that injures and a typhoon that levels the garden.

The story "Marta al-Baniyah," depicts a Beiruti prostitute as a victim of poverty and the cruelty of men rather than as an evil painted whore attempting to seduce upright citizens. Here appear several of Gibran's ethical convictions, which later shape Almustafa's discourse to the townspeople that fateful month of Ielool: that the god-self is ultimately immune to degradation, that evil deeds have origins that must be taken into account, that the adulterer's sin cannot be understood without looking at the behavior of the spouse, that regret is itself a more painful punishment than society could mete out.

"Yuhanna the Madman" is a story of the conflict of a poor peasant boy with the powerful Maronite

Catholic Church, and is probably loosely based on the life of an early nineteenth-century convert to Protestantism in Mount Lebanon, who was murdered by outraged Maronites. The narrative also recalls the revolt staged by Lebanon's long-suffering peasants against their rapacious landlords in 1858-1860. Gibran, himself from a relatively poor family in the village of Bisharri, clearly identified with and unreservedly supported the exploited peasants. His willingness openly to attack the elite that still dominated Mount Lebanon in his own day stirred a fire storm of public debate back home and caused his works to be censored or excluded from Ottoman Syria altogether. Yuhanna is a type of the prophet, who sees clearly through the façade of conventional mores to perceive the evil that sometimes lurks behind them, and denounces the hypocrisy of laws that impose steep penalties on poor dirt farmers for the slight damage done by their livestock to a wealthy monastery's vineyards. Yuhanna, like Almustafa, thinks that those who dress themselves up in morality in order to show it off would be better advised to practice nudity.

Although these stories are vital and accessible to Western readers, they retain some features that betray their Near Eastern origins. "The Ash of Centuries and the Immortal Flame" and "Marta al-Baniyah" depend for their dramatic effect upon a two-part symmetry, with an initial scene that contrasts dramatically to the second scene. This aesthetic of symmetry, with roots in Arabic literature, differs from the Western conception of a story as a narrative with a beginning, middle and end wherein the action is driven by the actions of the protagonist and their effects. It seems likely, as well, that Gibran's devotion to drawing and painting inspired him with a keen appreciation for the value of contrast, and led him to give us a series of diptychs, of paired, contrasting tableaux, each depicted in loving detail. "Yuhanna the Madman," on the other hand, comes much closer to the general Western story-telling model, with its series of conflicts between the protagonist and the monks, each driven by Yuhanna's own actions and psychological bent.

Despite his Lebanese origins and the influence on him of Arabic literature, from *A Thousand and One Nights* to the Koran and the Arabic Bible, Gibran is a quintessentially American writer, a celebrator of the individual, of progress, of initiative. Like Whitman, Gibran combines his faith in progress with a love of nature, and his belief in the individual with a mystical pantheism. Yet Gibran is a hyphenated American, and those now seeking evidence of creativity and achievement in U.S. writing by groups outside the WASP elite might reconsider him. The work he produced in the first half of his creative life is an American literature in Arabic; what could be more multicultural?

His works have all the hallmarks of an immigrant literature—the feelings of alienation, of falling between two stools, of new possibilities and rebellion against old rigidities. His is a Horatio Alger story of ascent from the Boston slums near Chinatown to the chic galleries of New York's intelligentsia in the roaring Twenties. Such an ascent exacts a price. Gibran's troubles with the Maronite Catholic Church resulting from his modern, American anticlericalism (seen here in "Yuhanna the Madman") are as old an immigrant story as the Pilgrims' problems with the Established English Church and as young a one as Salman Rushdie's difficulties with the ayatollahs. The immigrant finds it suddenly possible to experiment, not only with cultural forms, but also with values. Like Yeats, Gibran sought a pagan spirituality, engaged in meditative exercises, and believed in a vivid spirit world and in reincarnation. Gibran's rejection of organized religion and conventional morality while retaining an interest in spiritual growth is, again, very American.

Because of works such as these stories, Gibran occupies a far different place in Arabic literature than he does in American letters. The short story, as opposed to the traditional tale, was not an indigenous literary form in the Middle East, and writers there began experimenting with it only in the late nineteenth century, usually modelling themselves on European writers such as Maupassant. *Spirit Brides* is among the first widely read books of short stories in the Middle East, so that Gibran must be seen to some extent as a sort of Arabic-language Edgar Allen Poe. The Arabic-speaking writers living in the American diaspora (*al-mahjar*) had a profound effect on literature back in the Middle East, similar that of the Paris-based writers of the Lost Generation on the U.S. in the 1920s. In Arabic literature courses taught to the approximately 180 million native Arabic speakers world-wide, Gibran's works form part of the established literary canon, despite the occasional colloquialisms and grammatical idiosyncrasies in his writing that are the mark of his American experience and of his relatively limited formal education in Beirut.

Nor was working in the short story genre his only contribution. In an American context, Gibran was a neo-Romantic, influenced by Rousseau, Blake, Shelley, Whitman and Yeats, and by a selective reading of Nietzsche. The Romantic agony may have resonated especially well with the expatriate author's lived experience of homesickness and cultural ambiguity. In Arabic literature, however, there had been no Romantic movement in the nineteenth century. Partially because of the European colonial challenge to culture and politics, from the mid-nineteenth-century Middle Eastern authors had attempted to revive techniques and concerns of the golden age of the medieval Muslim Caliphate. Against this backdrop of Neoclassicism, the new sensibilities of Gibran and others were refreshing, sensitive, and vibrant, and his work helped provoke an unprecedented vogue for Romanticism that lasted three decades.

These stories often depicted a tragic hero opposing the hypocrisies of a culture mired in tradition, protesting against the treatment of women in a highly patriarchal society, the exploitation of the poor by the rich, and the vicissitudes of love. Students of modern Arabic literature have perceived a shift in the early twentieth century from fantastic and melodramatic tales of an episodic nature, centered on fate-driven heroic protagonists, toward realistic stories, often of victims, with more rounded characters and studies in psychological motivation. Social justice and some realist concerns become important.

This shift can be seen within *Spirit Brides* itself, as one moves from "The Ash of Centuries and the Immortal Flame" to "Yuhanna the Madman." Gibran is among those responsible for this reorientation. He also broke out of the confining classical style, developing a lovely prose poetry or poetic prose that employed delicate metaphors and similes and a taut concision of expression, inspiring many imitators, most of whom failed to reach his standard.

Gibran's Romanticism was increasingly wrought up with a sort of Syrian or Syro-Lebanese nationalism. His idyllic depiction of Seleucid Syria in "Ash of Centuries" as vibrant and affluent, in contrast to the poverty-stricken Arab herdsmen and peasants of the Bekaa valley in his own time, makes an incidental statement about past national glory and present decadence.

Without wanting to argue that there is necessarily a direct connection, I wish to point out that Naguib Mahfouz, the 1988 Nobel Laureate from Egypt, began his career in the 1930s writing Romantic nationalist novels in Arabic that were set in Pharaonic Egypt. There is therefore a thematic link, at least, between the Romantic revolution in Arabic letters that Kahlil Gibran helped launch and one phase in the career of Mahfouz, the writer who ultimately suc-

ceeded in making modern Arabic literature an inex-
tricable part of world literature.

Juan R. I. Cole
Ann Arbor, Michigan
6 August 1993

The Ash of Centuries
and the Immortal Flame

I
Initiation
(Autumn, 116 B.C.)

As night grew quiescent life sought repose in the City of the Sun,[C] and lamps were extinguished in the dwellings strewn around the mighty temples that nestled in groves of olive and laurel trees. The moon rose, spilling its rays upon white marble pillars that, looming like titans in the quiet of the night, stood guard over the sacrificial altars of the gods. The columns gazed with wonder and bewilderment toward the towers of Lebanon, perched among rocky debris on the ridges of faraway hills.

[C] The City of the Sun is Baalbek, that is, the City of Baal, the god of the sun. The ancients called it the City of the Sun or Heliopolis because it was built for the worship of this deity, and historians are agreed that it was the most beautiful city in Syria. As for the ruins that survive down to our day, most of them were built by the Romans after they had conquered Syria.

In that hour filled with magic stillness, wherein slumbering souls are united with their infinite dreams, Nathan, the son of the High Priest Hiram, arrived bearing a torch and entered into the temple of Astarte.[*] Hands trembling, he lit the lamps and ignited the thuribles within, sending the aroma of myrrh and frankincense spiralling upward. He arrayed the idol of the adored one with a translucent veil, resembling the shroud of hope that encompasses the human heart, then genuflected before the altar embellished with leaves of ivory and gold. He raised his hands and looked toward the heavens, and from his eyes flowed rivulets of tears that begat streams. He cried out, in a voice rendered faint by painful travails and broken by cruel lovesickness:

"Thy compassion, O supreme Astarte! Compassion, O goddess of love and beauty. Have mercy upon me and stay thou the hand of death from my beloved, whom my soul has chosen in accordance with thy will. The philters and potions of the physicians have fallen

---

[*] Astarte was a great goddess among the ancient Phoenicians, who worshipped her in Tyre and Sidon, in Jubayl and Baalbek. According to them, among her attributes are "igniter of the flame of life and guardian of youth." Greece borrowed her worship from the Phoenicians, calling her Aphrodite, the goddess of love and beauty, and the Romans called her Venus.

short and the incantations of the priests and mystics have proven false and impotent, and no helper or succorer is left to me save thy sanctified name. Hear then my entreaty, and see how my heart is crushed and my affections tormented. Keep the cynosure of my soul alive at my side, that we might rejoice in the mysteries of thy love and be gladdened by the beauty of youth that announces the secrets of thy splendor. I cry out to thee from these depths, O holy Astarte. From behind the gloom of this night I seek refuge in thy loving-kindness.

"Hearken to me, then, for I am thy servant, Nathan, the son of the priest Hiram, who has his entire life stood in service at thine altar. I fell in love with a girl and took her as my companion, but the brides of the spirits envied us and blew into her frail body the breath of a weird illness.ᶜ They dispatched the messenger of fate to convey her to their eldritch grottoes, and he lurks there even now beside her couch, raging like a ravenous leopard, his black wings billowing above her, stretching forth his rough talons that he might snatch her from my side.

ᶜ The Arabs of the pre-Islamic Age of Ignorance say that when a female genie falls in love with a young human she prevents him from marrying. If he should manage to do so, she ensorcels his bride or causes her to die, and these poetic beliefs still survive among some villages in Lebanon.

"For this reason have I come to thee, abasing myself. Be merciful and spare her, for she is a flower that has not yet delighted in the beauty of life's summer, a bird in the midst of her song celebrating the arrival of youth's dawn. Deliver her from the claws of death, and we shall revel in hymns of thy praise, devoting burnt offerings to the glory of thy name, performing blood sacrifices upon thy altar, filling up the vessels of thy storehouses with vintage wines and scented oils, carpeting the halls of thy temple with roses and jasmines, and lighting sweet-smelling incense and aloe before thy likeness. Save us, Mistress of Miracles, and permit love to vanquish death, for thou art goddess of death and love."

He fell silent for a moment, his agony descending in tears and rising in sighs. Then he resumed his plea, "My dreams lie in ruins, O holy Astarte, the spark of my life has faded, my heart has perished within me, and my eyes are aflame with burning tears. Revive me with thy tenderness and spare my beloved for me."

Suddenly, one of his slaves entered and slowly approached, whispering in his ear: "She opened her eyes, my lord, and glanced around her couch. When she did not see you, she called out your name insistently, so I came to summon you."

Nathan rose and strode rapidly, his slave following behind. When he reached his mansion he entered the patient's chamber and leaned over her bed, taking her slender hand, kissing her lips repeatedly as though attempting to inspire her ailing body with new life from his own. Her head sunk in silk pillows, she turned her face toward him and opened her lids slightly, then on her lips a phantom smile appeared, the remnant of life in her delicate frame, the last ray of her reposited soul, the echo from the cry of a heart hastening toward its own demise.

She spoke in a broken voice that recalled the gasps of a poor, hungry child: "The gods have sent for me, betrothed of my soul, and death has come to separate me from you. Do not sorrow, for the will of the gods is sacred and the demands of death are just. I am going now, for we no longer grasp the chalices of love and youth in our hands, and the splendid byways of life no longer stretch before us. I depart, darling, to the mead of souls, and shall come back to this world, for mighty Astarte returns to life the spirits of lovers꞉ who vanish

---

꞉ The Prophet of Islam, may peace be upon him, said: "You were dead and He brought you back to life, then He will cause you to die and revive you, then ye shall return unto him." The Buddha in India said: "Yesterday we were in this life and we have now come again, and we shall return until we become perfect like the gods."

into eternity without partaking in the bliss of love and the delights of youth. We shall meet, Nathan, and drink together the dew of morning from narcissus blossoms, and bask with the birds of the fields in the sunbeams. Until we meet again, my beloved."

Her voice trailed off, her lips trembling like a wilting flower shaken by dawn gales. Her lover gathered her up in his arms and his tears moistened her neck. When his lips approached her mouth, he found it ice cold, and he wailed in terror, ripping his tunic and flinging himself upon her lifeless body, his own anguished soul vacillating between the depths of life and the abyss of death.

In the quiet of that night, the eyelids of sleepers fluttered, the women of the quarter grew anxious, and children's minds were frightened when the garment of night was rent by excruciating shrieks and bitter weeping issuing from the mansion of the priest of Astarte.

When came the morn, the people sought out Nathan to solace and console him in his calamity, but they could discover him nowhere.

After a few days a caravan arrived from the east, the leader of which informed them that he had espied Nathan wandering in a far desert, out of his senses, in the haunts of gazelles.

∾

Ages passed, crushing beneath invisible feet the works of previous generations, and the gods grew remote from the land. Irascible deities took their place, who delighted in havoc and chaos. The stately temples of the City of the Sun were demolished, its striking palaces razed. Its lush gardens withered, and its fertile plots became barren. Nothing remained in that spot save decrepit ruins that called the specters of yesteryear painfully to mind and reminded the soul of the reverberations of ancient and magnificent jubilees.

But the eons that pass and crush the works of humans cannot annihilate their dreams or weaken their emotions.

Dreams and feelings survive with the endurance of the eternal, Universal Soul, though they might wane at times and subside at others, just as does the sun with the approach of night or the moon with the advent of the morn.

II

(Spring, 1,890 after the coming of Jesus the Nazarene)

The day dwindled, the light faded, and the sun gathered up its sash from the plains of Baalbek. Ali al-Husaini[c] returned at the head of his flock to the remains of the temple and seated himself amidst fallen pillars that resembled the ribs of an abandoned soldier, rent by combat and stripped by the elements. His sheep lay themselves down around him, seeking security in the melodies of his reed flute.

In the middle of the night the sky sowed the seeds of the morrow in the chasms of its blackness. Ali's eyelids wearied of the phantasms of wakefulness and his reason tired of the procession of apparitions that paced with eerie tranquillity among what remained of the walls. He made a pillow of his forearm, as drowsiness stole nigh and caressed his senses with the hem of its inmost veil, as the fog caresses the surface of a placid lake. He forgot his borrowed essence and encountered his hidden, archetypal spirit, brimming with

---

[c] The al-Husaini's are an Arab tribe that dwells in tents on the plains of Baalbek in our own day.

dreams that transcended the laws and teachings of human beings. The range of his vision widened before his eyes, concealed mysteries were revealed to him, and his soul withdrew from the pageant of time that was speeding toward oblivion. He stood alone before symmetrical thoughts and vying ideas, for the first time in his life knowing, or almost knowing, the reasons for the spiritual hunger that had overtaken his youth, a hunger that combined the sweetness with the bitterness of life, a thirst that united the sigh of yearning with the serenity of contentment, a craving that the splendors of this world could never remove nor the torrents of life divert.

For the first time in his life, Ali al-Husaini experienced an uncanny feeling, awakened in him by the relics of the temple. It was a delicate sentiment, the memory of where the incense had lain near the censers. It was an enchanted emotion that played over his senses the way a musician's fingers play over consecutive strings. The new feeling sprang forth from nothing, or from everything, growing and progressing until it embraced the entirety of his soul and filled it with an ardent passion tempered only by its gentleness, and with a grief sweet in its bitterness and delicious in its cruelty. The feeling was generated from within a single sleep-filled moment, and from a single moment are born the customs of generations, just as peoples propagate themselves from a single seed.

Ali glanced at the ruined temple, his drowsiness abruptly dissipating into an ethereal wakefulness. The remnants of the defaced altar appeared, the positions of the scattered pillars and crumbling foundations stood revealed. His gaze frozen, his heart fluttering, like a blind man regaining his sight, he began to see and think and contemplate. To think and contemplate. This round of surging thought and reflection generated in his soul the ghosts of a memory, then he remembered. He remembered these pillars standing proudly upright. He recalled silver lamps and thuribles ranged about a revered statuette. He remembered worthy priests offering up sacrifices before an altar embellished with leaves of ivory and gold. He called to mind young girls beating drums and youths chanting hymns to the goddess of love and beauty. He remembered and saw these lucid images with electrified vision, feeling the influence of their enigmas that stirred him to the depths. The memory, however, brought back only nebulous images, such as we see when we think back on our past life and hear only echoes of the voices our ears once perceived. What connection could there be between this mystic remembrance and the past life of a youth born among tents, who spent the spring of his life shepherding a flock in the countryside?

Ali rose and walked among the fallen stones, his distant memories pulling the veil of forgetfulness from his imagination as a little girl might brush a spider's web from the face of her mirror. When he reached the sanctuary of the temple he stood stock still, as though the earth's gravity had seized his feet. He looked around and found himself standing before a smashed sculpture which was sunk into the ground. He knelt next to it aimlessly, and emotion flooded his breast the way hemorrhaging blood rushes from a grave wound. His pulse quickened then slackened, just as the waves of the sea rise and fall. He lowered his eyes, sighing repeatedly, then wept tormentedly, for he felt a painful solitude, a poisonous distance, separating him from a beautiful spirit who had been close to him before his advent in this life.

He felt that the substance of his soul was only a spark taken from a brightly burning flame, which God had severed from his essence only a little before his life had ended.

He perceived the rustling of delicate wings, fluttering among his inflamed ribs and around his reeling brain.

He felt an ardent, powerful love encompass his heart and take control of his breathing, the love that divulges the secrets of the soul to the soul and by its poetics distinguishes true intellect from the realm of measurement and quantity. We hear that love speaking when the tongue of life falls silent, and see it as towering pillars of light when gloom envelops all things. That love, that god, descended at that hour upon the soul of Ali al-Husaini and awakened in him emotions both bitter and sweet, just as the sun causes flowers to blossom next to thorns.

Yet, what is this love, and whence has it come? What does it want of a shepherd boy among these decayed temples? What is this wine flowing in a breast that had never been moved by the sight of young girls? What is this celestial melody reverberating in the ears of a bedouin who had never yet delighted in the songs of women?

What is this love, and from where has it come? What does it want of Ali, distracted from the world by his sheep and his flute? Is it a seed cast by his bedouin virtues among the broken pieces of his heart without the knowledge of his senses? Or is it a ray of light that the mist had concealed, which has now become manifest, illuminating the recesses of his soul? Is it a dream striving in the tranquillity of the night to toy with his feelings, or is it a reality existing from all eternity, which will remain until the end of time?

Ali closed his tear-filled eyes and stretched out his hands like a supplicant seeking compassion. His spirit quaked within him incessantly, unleashing staccato sighs composed partly of abject suffering and partly ardent longing. In a voice indistinguishable from a sigh, save in the faint resonance of the words, he said:

"Who are you who are close to my heart, remote from my gaze, who separates me from myself and binds my present to a distant and forgotten past? Are you a vision, a houri come from the world of eternity to demonstrate to me the vanity of life and the frailty of human beings? Or the spirit of the queen of genies ascending from crevasses in the earth to dispossess me of my reason and make a fool of me among the youths of my tribe? Who are you, what is this captivation that grips my heart, which kills and then revives? What are these sensations that fill my bosom with light and fire? Who am I, and what is this new essence that I now call 'I,' though it be strange to me? Has the elixir of life been mixed with particles of ether, transforming me into an angel who sees and hears recondite mysteries? Or is this the wine of delusion on which I have become drunk, that has blinded me to the reality of intelligible things?"

He grew silent for a moment, then his feelings grew and his spirit rose, and he said: "You are the one whom the soul makes evident and to whom it draws near, whom the night disguises and sends far away. Beautiful spirit, who hovers in the heavens of my reveries, you have awakened within me feelings that lay dormant like flower bulbs buried beneath layers of snow. You passed by like a breeze bearing the scent of fields, and you brushed against my senses, which trembled like the twigs of a tree. Permit me to see you, if you are clothed in matter. Or pass by in my sleep, once it closes my eyes, that I might see you in a vision, if you are liberated from mortal clay. Let me feel your touch and listen to your voice. Rend this curtain that cloaks me in my entirety. Destroy this structure that veils my divinity, and grant me wings that I might soar beyond you to the mead of the heavenly host, if you be of its denizens. Or caress my eyes with enchantment and I will follow you to the hiding place of the genies, if you are one of their brides. Place your invisible hand upon my heart and possess me, if am worthy of being your devotee."

Ali whispered into the ears of the darkness his words, which followed the lilting melody echoing deep in his breast. Between his eyes and his surroundings, phantoms of the night proliferated like vapors given off by his hot tears, and on the walls of the temples appeared magical forms in all the colors of the rainbow.

In this manner an hour passed, as he rejoiced in his tears, delighting in his anguish, listening to the beating of his heart, gazing at what lay behind existing things as though the outlines of this life were slowly fading before his eyes, replaced by a dream wondrous in its charms, terrifying in its apprehensions. Like a prophet contemplating the stars in the heavens in expectation of being struck by a revelation, he awaited the arrival of each minute, his quick sighs interrupting his gentle breathing. His soul would leave him and swim about him, then return, as though it were searching among those ruins for a lost loved one.

ॳ

Dawn broke, disturbing the stillness with its breezes; violet light flooded through the ether, and the sky smiled mournfully. An apparition of his beloved appeared to him in a dream. Sparrows peeked out from the fissures in the walls, passing from one pillar to another and warbling their soliloquies, announcing the approach of day. Ali stood, placing his hand on his burning forehead. He looked around stiffly and, like Adam when the breath of God opened his eyes, he viewed everything he saw with wonder. He approached his ewes, calling them, and they rose, shook themselves, and walked behind him quietly toward verdant pastures. Ali preceded his flock, his eyes fixed on the cloudless sky. His feelings, now disconnected from his senses, made clear to him the mysteries and obscurities of being, showing him at a single glance what had passed away and what remained of bygone ages. In the wink of an eye they caused him to forget it all and restored to him an intense yearning. He found his essence veiled from his inmost spirit, as the eye is veiled from the light, and with each of his sighs a flame blazed forth from his burning heart.

He arrived at a brook that divulged by its purling the mysteries of the surrounding fields, and sat on its bank beneath willow branches that dangled above the water as though thirsting for a sip of its sweetness. His ewes bent down to graze on the grasses, the morning dew glistening against the white of their wool. A minute had not passed before he felt a quickening of his pulse and a renewed agitation of his spirit. Like a sleeper aroused by a playful sunbeam, he saw a girl appear from among the trees, carrying a jar on her shoulder and advancing slowly toward the creek, her naked feet moist with dew.

When she reached the edge of the stream and stooped to fill her jug, she glanced toward the other bank and found herself staring into Ali's eyes. With a slight moan, she threw down the vessel and edged back a bit, with the look of one who had been lost and then found a familiar face . . . A minute passed, each second a lamp guiding their hearts unto their hearts, weaving from the quietude exotic songs that recalled to their souls the echo of cryptic memories. They saw each other in a different place, surrounded by forms and phantoms distant from that brook and those trees. Each of them gazed at the other with tender affection, discovering comely features, listening to the other's sighs with all the intensity of which their emotions were capable, confiding in the other with all the eloquence of their spirits.

Finally, when their two souls had reached a state of complete understanding and intimacy, Ali crossed the stream, drawn by some indiscernible power. He approached the girl and embraced her, bestowing kisses upon her lips, then her neck, then her eyes. She barely stirred within his arms, as though the rapture of his embrace had sapped her of all will and the delicacy of his caress had deprived her of her faculties. She surrendered, as the perfumed breath of the jasmine submits to the buffeting wind. She dropped her head upon his breast like one exhausted, heaving a deep sigh that betrayed the relief her grief-stricken heart had found and announced the trembling of a bosom that had awakened from its slumber. She raised her head and looked into his eyes, signalling her disdain for the mere converse of humans in favor of a profound stillness—the language of spirits—and her displeasure with the idea that words could ever incarnate the essence of love.

The two lovers walked amid the willow grove. The oneness of each of them was a pair of lips declaring their unity, an ear listening to the revelations of their love, and an eye dazzled by the splendor of happiness. The lambs followed them, grazing upon the tips of grasses and flowers. Sparrows were arrayed before them on all sides warbling the songs of daybreak.

Thy reached the edge of the valley as the sun cast a golden robe on the surrounding hills. They sat near a boulder in whose shade a bed of violets had taken shelter. After a moment, the girl looked into Ali's two jet pupils while the breeze toyed with her hair, as though attempting to kiss her with unseen lips. She felt as though enchanted fingertips played about her tongue and lips against her will. She said, with a voice imbued with painful sweetness, "Astarte has returned our spirits to this world, lest we be deprived of the delights of love and the glories of youth, O my beloved!"

Ali closed his eyes as the music of her words made present to him the outlines of a dream he had repeatedly seen in his sleep. He felt as though invisible wings had lifted him from that place and deposited him in a strange room, near a bed on which lay the corpse of a beautiful woman that death had deprived of her luster and the warmth of her lips. He gave a scream of anguish at the horror of the scene, then opened his eyes and found that same girl sitting beside him, a smile of love on her lips, rays of life in her gaze. His countenance illumined, his spirit reinvigorated, he found that the specters of his vision faded. He forgot the past and its dead ends . . .

The two lovers embraced and drank the wine of their kisses until inebriated, and they slept in one another's arms until the shade receded and the sun's heat awakened them.

Marta al-Baniyah[1]

I

Her father perished while she yet lay in the cradle and her mother died before she reached ten, so she was left an orphan to be raised in the home of an impoverished neighbor. He lived, with his wife and children, off the fruits of the earth on an isolated farm amidst the splendid valleys of Lebanon.

Her father perished, bequeathing her naught save his name and a mean hovel among walnut and white poplar groves; and her mother died, leaving her nothing save tears of distress and the abasement of orphanhood. She remained destitute in the land of her birth, alone among those high boulders and dense coppices, every day making her way, barefoot and in tattered clothes, behind a milch cow toward a valley rich in

[1] This name derives from "Ban," a village in Lebanon

25

pasture. She would sit in the shade of branches, humming with songbirds, weeping to the purling of the brooks, envying the cow her grassy cornucopia, wistfully musing on the budding flowers and fluttering butterflies. When the sun set and hunger gnawed at her, she would return to her hut and sit with the little girl of her guardian, greedily tearing at a crust of millet bread with a little dried fruit and some legumes in vinegar and oil. Then she would sprawl on some parched straw, head resting on her forearms, and sleep, sighing, wishing all of life were a profound slumber uninterrupted by dreams and never ended by wakefulness. When dawn came, her guardian would chidingly awaken her to fulfill some wish of his, and she would leap up from her resting place, trembling with fright at his tantrums and his tirades.

Thus passed the years for penniless Marta, amidst those distant hills and valleys, and she grew up like a wild plant. In her heart emotions sprouted, just as nectar arises in the depths of a flower, and she encountered dreams and misgivings, rather as a herd crosses one rivulet, then another. She became a thoughtful girl, like good, virgin soil in which knowledge had not sown its seeds and upon which the feet of experience had not trodden. She possessed a great, pure soul, banished by the edict of fate to that farm where life changed with the seasons of the year, as though it were the shadow of an unknown god seated between heaven and earth.

We who spend the bulk of our lives in densely populated cities know virtually nothing of the lives of those who inhabit the secluded villages and farms of Lebanon. We have joined the tide of modern civilization, coming to forget or ignore the philosophy of that lovely, simple life filled with purity and goodness. Whenever we contemplate that life, we find it radiant in the springtime, heavy laden in the summer, fruitful in the fall, cozy in the winter. It resembles Mother Nature in all her phases. We exceed the villagers in our wealth, but they are more noble than we in their souls; we sow much but reap nothing, while they harvest whatever they sow. We are slaves to our ambitions, while they are children of their contentment. We imbibe the elixir of life mixed with bitterness, despair, fear, and ennui, whereas they drink it pure.

Marta reached the age of sixteen and her soul became like a polished mirror that reflecting the virtues of the open fields, while her heart resembled the empty spaces in the gullies that return the echo of every sound . . . On a fall day that resounded with the sighs of nature, she sat near a spring that had been liberated from the earth's prison, just as thoughts strive free of the poet's imagination. She contemplated the trembling of yellowed leaves upon the trees, the way the wind toyed with them, so like the manner in which death plays with human souls. She looked at the flowers, finding that they had wilted and withered to the core and had burst apart, entrusting their seeds to the earth the way women do their jewelry in times of war and revolution.

While gazing at the flowers and trees, feeling with them the ache of summer's departure, she heard the sound of hoof beats on the gravel at the bottom of the gully. She looked around and discovered a horseman slowly approaching her. He drew near the spring, his features and clothing suggesting a certain wealth and style. He dismounted from his charger and hailed her with a courtesy she had in no wise come to expect from a man.

He asked her, "I've wandered from the road that leads to the coast. Can you guide me to it, girl?"

Standing straight as a branch on the edge of a spring, she answered, "I don't rightly know, sir. But I'll go and ask my guardian, who does know."

She spoke the words with obvious anxiety, and her bashfulness lent her a certain beauty and delicacy. When she rose to depart, the man stopped her, the wine of youth flowing in his veins, his gaze abruptly altering.

"No," he said. "Don't go."

She stood rooted to the spot, bewildered, conscious of a power in his voice that prevented her from moving. When she timidly stole a glance at him, she saw that he was contemplating her with an interest she could not understand and smiling with an enchanting kindness that, in its sweetness, nearly brought tears to her eyes. He was gazing with love and affection at her naked feet, her lovely wrists, her smooth neck, and her thick, soft hair. He mused, enthralled and infatuated, upon the way the sun had tanned her complexion and nature had given strength to her forearms. As for the girl, her head bowed with shyness, she did not want to leave but she could not speak, for reasons that escaped her.

That evening, the milch cow came back alone to the corral, but Marta did not return. When her guardian arrived from his fields, he searched for her among those ravines, but did not find her. He called her name, but his only reply came from the caves and the sighing of the wind among the trees. He returned, sorrowful, to his shack and informed his wife, who wept softly the entire night. She said to herself, I saw her once in a dream, caught in the talons of a savage beast that shredded her body as she smiled and sobbed.

That is, in brief, what I knew of Marta's life on that lovely farm. I heard it from an elderly villager, who knew her from the time she was a little girl until her adolescence, when she vanished from that place. She left behind her only a few tears in the eyes of her guardian's wife and a fragile, affecting memory that wafts with the breezes of morning in that gorge, then fades like the breath of a child on a window pane.

II

The autumn of 1900 arrived and I returned to Beirut, having spent the summer recess in the north of Lebanon. Before starting classes, I passed an entire week wandering about with my comrades in the city, enjoying the bliss of freedom that youth so loves and which it is denied at home and in the classroom. We resembled so many sparrows who spied the door of their cage open before them, so they proceed to sate their hearts with the delight of roaming wild and the rapture of warbling their songs. Youth is a delicious dream, the savor of which is stolen by the riddles of textbooks that render it a harsh vigil. Will ever a day come when sages can combine the reveries of youth with the joys of learning, the way a common enemy unites the hearts of those who hate one other? Will a time arrive when nature becomes the teacher of the son of Adam, and humanity his book, and life his school? We do not know. But we sense our rapid progress toward spiritual advancement, and that advancement is the perception of the beauty of natural things by means of our inmost feelings, and seeking happiness through our love for that beauty.

One evening, I was sitting on the balcony of the house, contemplating the constant struggle in the city square and listening to the hawking of the street vendors, each calling out the virtues of his wares or produce. A five-year-old boy approached, wearing tattered rags and hauling on his shoulders a tray of layered flowers. In a thin voice quelled by ingrained abasement and a pained, broken spirit, he said, "Want to buy a flower, mister?"

I looked into his small, sallow face, and pondered his eyes, with their dark circles, the mascara of poverty and wretchedness, his slightly open mouth like a deep wound in a pained countenance, his bare, skinny wrists, his slight, haggard frame, stooped beneath the tray of flowers, like the wilted stalk of a yellow rose amidst high grass. I mulled over all these sights in an instant, demonstrating my sympathy with smiles more bitter than tears, the sort of smiles that are torn from our inmost hearts and appear upon our lips and that, were we to leave them alone, would rise and spill forth from the corners of our eyes. So I bought some of his flowers, with the desire of purchasing his conversation. I sensed that behind his doleful glances lay a small heart, which enfolded within itself one act in the tragedy of the poor that is forever played out on the stage of days, but in which few take an interest because it is painful. When I addressed a few kind comments to him, he felt secure and friendly and looked at me with amazement because, like his companions among the poor, he was unused to anything but coarse words from those who, for the most part, view street boys as dirty things of no moment rather than as small, injured souls wronged by fate.

I asked him, then, "What's your name?"

He answered, his eyes lowered toward the ground, "My name is Fuad."

"Whose son are you, and where is your family?"

"I am the son of Marta al-Baniyah," he said.

"Where is your father?"

He shook his little head, as though ignorant of the meaning of the word "father."

I said, "Where is your mother, Fuad?"

"Sick at home."

My ears drank in these few words from the boy's mouth and my emotions lapped them up, creating uncanny, melancholic images and phantoms, since I knew in a second that Marta the pauper, whose story I had heard from the villager, at that moment lay ill in Beirut. The girl who had only yesterday enjoyed safety among the trees of the valleys today suffered the tor-

ments of poverty and heartache in the city. The orphan who had passed her youth in the palm of nature,
herding cattle in lovely fields, had descended along
the bank of the river to the corrupt city and become
prey to the claws of misery and distress.

While I was thinking and imagining these things,
the boy was looking at me as though he saw by the eye
of his pure soul how my heart was crushed.

When he started to depart, I grabbed his hand
and said, "Take me to your mother. I want to see her."

He went before me, silent and perplexed. From
time to time he glanced back to see if I was really following in his footsteps.

In those grubby alleys where the air ferments with
the gasps of death, among those decrepit buildings
where felons commit their crimes, hiding behind cur-
tains of gloom, and in those winding back alleys that
bend first to the right and then to the left like black
vipers, I made my way in fear and dread. The boy before me possessed, by virtue of his youth and purity
of heart, a rare courage. But no one would share it
who knew the cunning ruses that the toughs practice
in this city, a city that Easterners call the Bride of Syria
and the jewel in the diadem of emperors. When we
arrived in the worst neighborhood, the boy entered a

shoddy dwelling, of which the years had left only one rickety wall intact. I entered, following behind him, my pulse accelerating as I drew near. I stood in the middle of a humid room bare of furniture except for a dim lamp that battled total blackness by the spears of its yellow rays and a dilapidated bed that bespoke agonizing penury and abject privation. Prostrate upon it lay a woman sleeping. She had turned her face to the wall, as though seeking protection thereby from the injustices of this world, or as though she found in it a heart more tender and empathetic than the hearts of human beings.

The boy approached her, calling, "Mama!"

She turned toward him and he pointed in my direction. She moved under the shabby blanket, and in a pained voice accompanied by soulful anguish and bitter sighs, she said, "What do you want, man? Are you here to buy my last days of life, to defile them with your cravings? Leave me! The alleyways are crowded with women who will peddle to you their bodies and souls for a trifle. As for me, I have nothing left to sell, except a few remaining uneven breaths. Soon, death will obtain them for the price of a quiet grave!"

I moved near to her bed. Her words had injured my heart, for they summed up her wretched story. I said, hoping that my emotions would flow with my words, "Don't be afraid of me, Marta. I have not come to you like a hungry animal, but as a distressed human being. I am a Lebanese, who lived for a while in those valleys and hamlets near the cedar forest. Don't fear me, Marta!"

She listened to my words and discerned that they had issued from the depths of a soul who shared her pain. She trembled on her bed like a bare twig before a winter tempest, covering her face with her hands as though she wanted to veil her essence from a memory terrifying in its sweetness, acrid in its comeliness. After a period of calm, rent by sighs, her face appeared above her trembling shoulders, and I saw sunken eyes fixed on an invisible object planted in the middle of the room, dry lips trembling with the convulsions of despair, a throat in which a death rattle sounded alongside a deep, intermittent moan.

She said, in a voice suffused with pleading and earnest supplication and reverberating with weakness and pain, "You have come with sympathy and good wishes, and may Heaven reward you—if doing good to sinners is a virtue and showing mercy to the wicked is a good deed. But I beg you, go back where you came from, since being recognized in this place will earn you only shame and criticism, and your kindness to me will get you only contempt and disgrace. Go back, before someone sees you in this grimy room splattered with the filth of pigs. Go, quick, and hide your face with your clothing to keep passersby from seeing who you are. The compassion that fills your soul cannot get back my purity for me, or erase my offenses, or keep the firm hand of death away from my heart. I've been exiled because of my sins to these gloomy depths, so don't let your pity bring you near to vice. I'm like a leper living in a graveyard, and you must not come near because society will consider you unclean and condemn you if you do. Go on back, now, and don't mention my name in those holy valleys, since the shepherd rejects the mangy ewe out of fear for his flock. When you mention me, say 'Marta al-Baniyah has died.' Don't say anything else."

She took her son's two small hands in hers and kissed them with a sigh, then said anxiously, "People will look on my son with ridicule and contempt, saying 'This is the yield of sin, this son of Marta the adulteress, this son of disgrace, this son of chance.' They'll say more than that about him, too, because they're blind and don't see, and ignorant and don't know. His mother has purified his childhood with her agony and her tears, and ransomed his life by her hardships and misery. I will die and leave him an orphan among the boys of the alley, alone in this harsh life. I will leave him nothing but a horrible memory. It will fill him with shame if he grows up weak and cowardly, and it will set his blood on fire if he's brave and just. If heaven keeps him safe he will grow up to be a strong man, a right hand of heaven against the one who wronged him and his mother. And if he should then die and escape from the web of years, he'll find me waiting for him where there's plenty of light and rest."

I spoke as my heart inspired me, saying, "You are not like a leper, Marta, even if you have dwelt among tombs, and you are not unclean, even if life has given you into the hands of the unclean. The body's filth cannot touch the pure soul, and snow drifts cannot destroy living seeds. This life is but a threshing floor of sorrows in which souls have their adversities sifted out before they give their yield. But woe unto the spikes of grain left outside the threshing floor, for the ants of the earth will carry them away and the birds of the sky will glean them, and they shall not enter the granary of the field's owner. You are oppressed, Marta, and the one who wronged you is the owner of mansions, the possessor of great wealth and a small soul. You have been wronged and scorned, but it is better for a human being to be oppressed than to be an oppressor, and more virtuous to be a martyr to the weakness of earthly impulses than to be a powerful person who crushes the flowers of life in his grasp and disfigures the noblest of emotions by his lusts.

"The soul, Marta, is a golden ring detached from the chain of divinity. Intense fire assays this ring and transforms its appearance, effacing the beauty of its roundness; but it cannot dissolve the gold into some other element, and only succeeds in burnishing it. Woe to the chaff, however, if the fire comes and devours it, reducing it to ash, which the winds scatter upon the face of the desert . . . Marta, you are a flower crushed beneath the feet of animals in human guise. Those soles trampled upon you cruelly, but could not conceal your fragrance, which ascended with the cries of the widows and the wailing of orphans and the sighs of the poor to heaven, the source of justice and mercy. Take comfort that you are a crushed flower and not a trampling foot."

I was talking and she was listening, and my consoling words illumined her pallid face the way the gentle rays of the setting sun light up the interior of clouds. She gestured to me that I should sit next to

4

the bed. I did so, scrutinizing her features, which spoke
of the woeful mysteries of her soul, the features of one
who knew she was dying; the features of a girl in the
springtime of her life who sensed death's footfalls
about her shabby bed; the features of a woman abandoned who yesterday walked among the splendid valleys of Lebanon filled with life and power, who today
awaited, haggard and wasted, her release from the
chains of life.

After an affecting pause, she gathered up the remnants of her faculties and said, while her tears echoed
and her soul ascended with her sighs, "Yes, I am one
wronged, a martyr to beasts dressed as men, a flower
smashed beneath their feet. I was sitting on the edge
of that spring when a horseman came by . . . He spoke
to me with kindness and tenderness and said I was
beautiful, that he loved me and would never leave me,
that the wild animals roamed the open country and that
jackals and birds of prey infested the valley . . . Then he
grabbed me and pressed me to his chest and kissed
me. I, an abandoned orphan, had never tasted a kiss
till that moment. He sat me behind him on the back
of his steed and brought me to a beautiful, isolated
house. He gave me silk dresses, refined perfumes,
choice meals, and rare wines . . . He did all that with a

And now, the hour has drawn near and the bridegroom of death has come, after his long separation, to lead me to my tender resting place."

After a profound calm, like the caress of spirits in flight, she raised her eyes, veiled in the shadow of hope, and said quietly, "Hidden Justice, concealed behind these terrifying images, you hear the lamentation of my soul, now commended to God, and the cry of my negligent heart. From you alone I ask and you I implore, have mercy and train my son with your right hand, and receive my spirit with your left."

Her strength faded and her sighs grew faint. She looked at her son with a mournful, pitying gaze. Her eyes slowly closed, and in a voice that approximated silence she said, "Our Father, who art in heaven, hallowed be thy name. Thy kingdom come, thy will be done, on earth as it is in heaven. Forgive us our trespasses . . ."

Her voice broke off, though her lips still worked for a while. When they stopped, all movement in her body faded away. Then she quivered and moaned, and her face drained of color, and her spirit emanated forth. Her eyes continued to stare at what could not be seen.

☙

When dawn came, the body of Marta al-Baniyah was placed in a wooden coffin, lifted up by two indigent pall-bearers, and buried in an abandoned field far from the city. The priests declined to pray over her remains, refusing to allow her bones to rest in any cemetery where the cross stands sentinel over the tombs. No one escorted her to that distant grave site save her son and another young man whom life's misfortunes had taught compassion.

Yuhanna the Madman

I

In the days of summer, Yuhanna made his way every morning to his fields, driving his steers and calves before him, carrying his plow on his shoulders, and listening to the songs of thrushes and the rustling of leaves on their branches. Around noon, he approached the irrigation ditch running amid the depressions in those verdant meadows, and ate his lunch, leaving the leftover bread on the grass for the sparrows. In the evening, when the sunset snatched particles of light from space, he returned to his humble abode high above the villages and farms of northern Lebanon. He would sit peacefully with his elderly parents, giving ear to their accounts of the olden days, feeling the close approach of both sleep and rest.

In the days of winter he leaned over the fire, warming himself, listening to the moaning of the wind and the wailing of the elements, meditating on the succession of seasons, looking out from his peephole of a window upon snow-covered vales and naked trees that resembled nothing so much as a horde of beggars abandoned to the clutches of the biting cold and powerful gusts.

During the long nights he stayed up until his father slept, then opened a wooden cabinet and took out the New Testament, reading from it secretly by the feeble light of a lamp. He cast a wary eye from time to time on his slumbering father, who had forbidden him to read that book because the priests forbade the simple of heart to delve into the secrets of Jesus's teaching, and withheld from them the blessings of the Church should they do so.

Thus Yuhanna passed his youth between beautiful fields, wondrous and the book of Jesus, brimming with light and spirit. Taciturn and contemplative, he listened to the conversation of his parents but gave no answer. He met with his youthful friends and sat with them quietly, peering into the distance, where the gloaming met the dark blue sky. When he went to church he returned dejected, for the teachings he heard from the pulpits and altars differed from what he read in the Gospel, and the lives of the believers with their leaders differed from the beautiful life about which Jesus of Nazareth had spoken.

∾

Spring came and the snow cover faded from the fields and leas, and even its remnants on the mountain peaks melted, flowing into streams in winding ravines and gathering into full rivers that roared out that nature had awakened. Almond and apple trees came into bloom, twigs of white poplar and willow put out their leaves, and knolls grew their grasses and flowers. Yuhanna tired of sitting next to the hearth, and he knew that his calves had grown bored of being penned up in the corral and yearned for green pastures, for the bales of straw had run low and the baskets of grain were exhausted. He went and freed them from their feedstalls and led them into the open country, concealing beneath his cloak a copy of the New Testament, that no one might see it. He reached the meadow spread out on the mountain slope above the gorge, near to the fields of a monastery᷎ that stood like an awesome tower among those hills. His calves scattered, grazing on the grass, while he sat leaning against a boulder, meditating at one time on the beauty of the valley and at another on verses of his book, which spoke of the kingdom of the heavens.

That afternoon was one of the last days of the fast. The inhabitants of those villages were abstaining from meat and were eagerly anticipating, with the last remnants of their patience, the arrival of Easter. As for Yuhanna, like the rest of the destitute peasants he made no distinction between days of fasting and other days, for his life was one long fast. His fare never exceeded a crust of bread leavened with the sweat of his brow and some fruit bought with the blood of his heart. He naturally abstained from meats and delicacies, so that the pleasures of fasting were not bodily but emotional, for they reminded him of the passion of the Son of Man and the end of his life on earth.

᷎ This is a wealthy monastery in the north of Lebanon, possessing extensive land, called Dayr Elyusha᷎ an-Nabi ("The Monastery of Elisha the Prophet"), wherein dozens of monks dwell, who are known as "Aleppines."

Sparrows fluttered, whispering around Yuhanna. A flock of doves hurriedly took flight, and the flowers bowed with the breeze as though sunning themselves in the daylight, while he became engrossed in reading his book. He looked up and saw the domes of the churches in the scattered cities and villages to either side of the valley, listening to the peal of their bells. He closed his eyes, and his soul floated above the generations to ancient Jerusalem, following the footsteps of Jesus in the streets, asking passersby about him.

They replied, "Here the blind were healed and the lame walked. Here they wove for him a crown of thorns and placed it on his head. In this quarter of the city, he halted and spoke to the masses in parables, and in that palace they shackled him to a column, spat in his face, and flogged him. In this street he forgave the sinful adulteress, and in that he fell to the earth under the weight of his cross."

An hour passed, as Yuhanna shared in the bodily pain of the God-man and was glorified with him in spirit, until midday, when he rose from his place and glanced around him in search of his calves. He did not see them. He walked around, looking in every direction, bewildered at their disappearance from that flat meadow. He reached the road that meandered between the fields like the lines of one's palm, and descried in the distance a man in black attire standing among the gardens. He hastened toward him, and recognized him, when he drew near, as one of the monks of the monastery.

He greeted him with a nod of his head and asked, "Have you seen calves wandering among these gardens, father?"

The monk looked at him, striving to conceal his exasperation, and replied maliciously, "Yes, I saw them. They are over there—come and I'll show you."

Yuhanna followed the monk until they reached the monastery, where he spied the calves in a huge corral, hobbled with ropes and guarded by one of the monks, who beat them with a stick whenever they moved. When Yuhanna made as if to lead them away, the monk seized him by his woolen wrap, then turned toward the living quarters of the monastery and shouted, "Here's the delinquent herder—I've detained him!"

Priests and monks came running from every direction, their abbot at their head. He stood out from his colleagues by virtue of the fineness of his clothing and his sour mien. They surrounded Yuhanna like soldiers competing for their prey. Yuhanna looked at their leader and said quietly, "What have I done, to be called a delinquent, and why have you grabbed hold of me?"

The abbot replied, his anger imbuing his face with cruelty, in a coarse voice resembling nothing so much as the screeching of a saw, "You pastured your calves in the monastery's standing crop, and they chewed the leaves of its vineyards. We have detained you because the herder is responsible for the damage caused by his animals."

Yuhanna beseeched them, "They are beasts lacking in reason, father, and I am a poor man possessing nothing but my strong right arm and these calves. Let me lead them away, and I promise you that I will never again return to these meadows."

The superior, having taken a step forward, lifted his hands to the heavens and said, "Verily, God has placed us here and made us stewards of these lands of his chosen one, the mighty Elisha. We safeguard them day and night with all our power, for they are sacred— they are like fire that consumes all who approach them. Were you to be unable to settle your account with the monastery, what your calves have eaten would turn to poison in their stomachs. But there is no question of your defaulting, as we shall keep your animals in our corral until you pay the last penny."

The abbot made as if to go, but Yuhanna stopped him, imploring him abjectly, "I beg you, my lord, by these holy days wherein Jesus suffered and Mary wept for our sorrows, to let me take away my calves. Do not be hardhearted toward me, for I am poor and destitute and the monastery is rich and glorious, and it will overlook my negligence and have compassion on the advanced age of my father."

The leader turned to him and mocked him, "The monastery will not forgive you one iota, ignoramus, whether you be rich or poor! Do not invoke holy things with me, for we know more than you about their enigmas and mysteries. If you wish to lead your calves out of this pen, then redeem them by paying three dinars in return for our crops that they devoured."

Yuhanna said, nearly choking, "I do not have a single cent, father. Show me compassion, and have mercy on my poverty."

The head monk ran his fingers through his thick beard. "Go and sell some of your land and come back with three dinars. It is better for you to enter heaven without land than to earn the wrath of Elisha by your protests before his altar and, in the next life, be cast down into Gehenna's everlasting fire."

Yuhanna fell silent for a moment, then his eyes flashed, his face gladdened, and signs of power and will replaced his expression of supplication. His voice blended the melody of knowledge with the determination of youth: "Should a poor man sell his fields, the source of his bread and mainstay of his life, in order to add its price to the treasury of a monastery already overflowing with silver and gold? Is it just that the poor should become poorer and the destitute should die of hunger, lest the mighty Elisha not forgive the sins of hungry beasts?"

The abbot shook his head haughtily, "Thus saith Jesus the Christ: 'To every one who has, more will be given, but from him who has not, even what he has will be taken away from him.'"[RSV]

Yuhanna heard these words, which disturbed his heart in his breast, and his soul grew, and his statur increased, as though the earth had risen beneath h feet.

He extricated the Gospel from his pocket, a soldier unsheathes his sword to defend himself, cried out, "Thus do you play with the teaching this book, hypocrites! Thus do you employ the ho thing in life to increase the evils of life. Woe unt when the Son of Man comes again and destroys monasteries and throws down their walls in this valley, burning with fire your altars and rituals and statues! Woe unto you for the innocent blood of Jesus and the pure tears of his Mother when a flood comes upon you and sweeps you into the deepest pit! Woe, a thousand times woe unto you, adorers of the idols of your banquets, you who conceal by your black cloaks the blackness of your hatreds, you who move your lips in prayer while your hearts are hard as stone, you who kneel humbly before the altar while your souls are rebelling against God. You have charged me with defiling this place that is filled with your sins, and have seized me like a criminal for the sake of a tiny part of your crop, which the sun causes to grow for me and for you alike. And when I beseeched you in the name of Jesus and invoked the days of his sorrows and passion, you mocked me as though I spoke nothing but foolishness and ignorance. Take this book and search in it and show me when Jesus refused to show mercy. Read this heavenly tragedy and inform me of where he spoke with other than compassion and graciousness. Is it in his sermon on the mount, or in his teachings in the temple before the persecutors of the poor adulteress, or on Golgotha when he stretched out his arms on the cross to embrace the human race?

"Look, you hardhearted monks, at these dirt-poor villages and towns. In their houses the sick writhe on beds of agony, in their jails the wretched watch their days vanish, before their doors beggars plead, on their streets the poor sleep, and in their graveyards widows and orphans lament. Meanwhile, you here enjoy the ease of loafing about in your albs, and revel in the fruits of your fields and the wines of your vineyards. You do not visit the sick or prisoners, or feed the hungry, or house the poor, or cheer the forlorn. Would that you contented yourselves with what you have, and made do with what you usurped from our grandfathers by your ruses. But you strike with your hands the way a snake strikes with its fangs, and use force to deprive the widow of what she has earned with her own two hands, and what the peasant has stored up for his old age."

Yuhanna fell silent as he regained his breath, then raised his head with pride and said quietly, "You are many here, and I am alone. Do with me what you wish. For wolves prey on the ewe in the dark of night, but the traces of her blood remain on the pebbles of the valley until the dawn arrives and the sun rises."

Yuhanna's voice, as he spoke, exhibited a sublime power that immobilized the bodies of the monks and provoked rage and fury in their souls. Like ravens in a cage, they trembled with anger and gnashed their teeth, scrutinizing their superior for a signal to rend him limb from limb and crush him into powder. When he had finished speaking, a quiet ensued like the calm after a storm has broken off lofty branches and dry trunks.

Their leader shrieked at them, "Seize that wretched criminal, confiscate his book, and drag him to a darkened room in the monastery! Whoso blasphemes against the chosen of God shall not be forgiven either here or in the hereafter."

The monks attacked Yuhanna like jackals assaulting their quarry, and they led him, bound, to a narrow cell, locking the door after they had worn down his body with harsh blows from their hands and kicks from their feet.

In that gloomy room Yuhanna stood, like a long-time victor whom the enemy had finally managed to capture, and looked out from the long, narrow aperture on the valley full of the light of day. His visage glowed, and he felt a spiritual rapture embrace his soul and a sweet serenity that possessed his emotions. The confining cell imprisoned only his body, whereas his soul remained at liberty, billowing with the breeze between hill and meadow. The hands of the monks, which inflicted pain on his members, had not touched his emotions, which were safeguarded in the precincts of Jesus of Nazareth. If a man be just, no persecution can torture him, and no tyranny can destroy him if he has right on his side. Socrates drank down his hemlock with a smile on his face, and Paul rejoiced while being stoned. But it is our hidden conscience that pains us if we violate it, and condemns us if we betray it.

Yuhanna's parents learned of what had befallen their only child, and his mother walked to the monastery, leaning on her cane. She threw herself at the feet of the abbot, shedding tears and kissing his hand that he might have mercy on her son and excuse his ignorance.

He replied to her, after lifting his eyes toward heaven like one exalted above earthly things, "We forgive your son's rashness and are prepared to be magnanimous toward his madness. But the monastery has sacred claims that must be settled. We pardon, by reason of our humility, the missteps of the people, but mighty Elisha does not forgive those who damage his vineyards and let their livestock pasture in his standing crops."

The mother gazed at him, tears flowing down her time-shriveled cheeks. Then she tore a silver necklace from her neck and placed it in his hand, saying, "I own nothing but this necklace, father. It was a gift from my mother on my wedding day. Let the monastery accept it as a ransom for the sins of my only child."

The abbot pocketed the necklace, then, while Yuhanna's mother kissed his hand with gratitude and indebtedness, he said, "Woe unto this generation, for therein the verses of the Book have been reversed: the children eat unripe grapes and the fathers' teeth are set on edge. Go, pious woman, and pray for your insane son, that heaven might heal him and return him to his senses."

Yuhanna departed from his captivity and walked slowly before his calves, next to his mother, who bent over her cane beneath the weight of her years. When he reached the hut, he guided the calves to their feed stalls and sat silently next to the window, meditating on the waning light of day. After a little while he heard his father whisper in his mother's ear, "How often you used to dispute with me, Sarah, when I said to you that your son is emotionally disturbed. Now I don't see you protesting, since his deeds have proven me right. The dignified head of the monastery himself told you today what I've been saying for years."

Yuhanna kept on looking west, where the rays of the sun were tinting the heavy cloud cover.

II

The holy day of Easter came, and otherworldliness was traded for feasts of delectable foods. The building had been completed of a new, lofty cathedral set among the dwellings of the city of Bisharri, like the palace of a prince standing among his subjects' shacks. The people were awaiting the arrival of one of the bishops to dedicate it and to consecrate its altar. When they heard that he was approaching, they issued in droves into the street and brought him into the city amidst the cheering of the youth, the praises to God voiced by the priests, the clash of cymbals, and the chiming and pealing of bells. When he dismounted from his horse, which had been caparisoned a brocaded saddle and furnished with a silver bridle, the notables and leaders greeted him with pleasant words, reciting poems and lyrics that began with praise and concluded with accolades. When he reached the new house of worship, he pulled on his priestly robes, embroidered with gold, placed on his head a miter inlaid with gems, and grasped the shepherd's staff, embellished with rare designs and precious stones. He circumambulated the temple, chanting prayers and formulas of consecration with the priests, as the pleasing aroma of incense rose all about him and a multitude of candles coruscated.

Yuhanna stood, at that hour, among the peasants and farmers, on a high roof, pondering the scene sadly, bitterly sighing, a painful lump in his throat. On one side he saw ornamented silk clothes, jewel-studded gold vessels, extravagant silver censers and braziers, on the other a mass of the poor and destitute who had come from small villages and farms to witness the gaiety of this Easter and to celebrate the consecration of the church. On one side, grandeur robed in velvet and satin, and on the other, misery wrapped in worn and tattered rags. Here stands a powerful, wealthy faction representing religion with its chants and praises, and there stands a weak and despised people rejoicing in their souls at the resurrection of Jesus from the dead and silently praying, whispering into the ears of the ether hot sighs that issue from the depths of broken hearts. Here stand chiefs and authorities, whose power bestows on them lives resembling cypress trees that remain green all year round. There stand paupers and peasants, whose submissiveness makes their lives like a ship, captained by death, its rudder broken upon the waves, its sails shredded by fierce gales, tossed between plunging troughs and rising crests, between the

wrath of watery chasms and the horror of the tempest. Here stands cruel tyranny, there blind obedience.
Which generated the other, then? Is despotism a strong
tree that can grow only in depressed lowlands, or is
deference an abandoned field wherein only thorns can
flourish?

Yuhanna busied himself with these painful ideas
and tormenting thoughts. Meanwhile, he folded his
forearms across his upper chest, his throat so constricted
that he had trouble getting his breath and feared that
his breast would be rent asunder, throat, trachea, and
all. When the consecration festivities ended, and the
people began to depart and scatter, he felt as though a
spirit in the air was giving him a commission and ex-
horting him. In the crowd was a power that galvanized
his soul and appointed him to speak before the heavens and the earth, a prisoner of his will.

He advanced to the side of the roof, lifting his
eyes and gesturing with his hand toward the firma-
ment, and in a powerful voice that caught the ear and
attracted stares, he shouted: "Look, O Jesus of
Nazareth, seated in the center of the most high circle
of light! Peer behind the azure dome at this earth, in
the elements of which you attired yourself only yesterday. See, Faithful Guardian, how the thorns of the

wilderness have choked the flowers, whose seeds take root through the sweat of your brow. Look, Good Shepherd, for the talons of savage beasts have pierced the side of the hapless lamb, which you had carried upon your shoulders. Look, for your pure blood has seeped into the earth, your hot tears have dried in the hearts of humankind, your warm breaths have perished before the desert winds. This field, which your own feet have blessed, has become a killing field wherein the hooves of the strong crush the ribs of the despised, and the claws of oppressors have plucked the soul from the weak . . .

"The cry of the wretched ascends from the very precincts of that gloom, and yet no one among those sitting on thrones in your name hears it; the lamentation of the sorrowful does not reach the ears of those who speak of your teachings at the pulpit. The lambs that were sent for the sake of the word of life have changed into wolves whose fangs rend the flanks of those sheep that you hugged with your own arms. The words of life that you revealed from the breast of God have been hidden in books, and their place has been taken by a terrifying clamor from which souls recoil, trembling, in dread.

"Jesus, they have raised for the glorification of their own names churches and cathedrals, adorning them with woven silk and refined gold, leaving the bodies of your chosen ones, the poor, naked in icy alleyways. They have filled the atmosphere with the fumes of incense and the flames of candles, and left the stomachs of the believers in your divinity empty of bread. They have crowded the air with chants and praises, but heard not the cry of the orphan or the sobs of the widow.

"Come again, Jesus the Living, and expel the merchants of religion from your temple, for they have reduced it to a grotto where vipers invent their tricks and chicanery. Come and call these Caesars to account, for they have pilfered what belongs to the weak and to God. Come, and look at the vineyards that you planted with your own right hand, for worms have eaten their stems and vagabonds have crushed their bunches of grapes. Come and look at those you entrusted with the peace, for they have divided into factions and become enemies of one another and warred amongst themselves, and the casualties of their war were none other than our sorrowing souls and our exhausted hearts.

"In their feast days and celebrations they boldly raise their voices, saying, 'Glory be to God in the highest, and on earth, peace, and to the people, joy.' But does it honor your heavenly Father for his name to be pronounced by sinful lips and lying tongues? And is there peace on earth when the children of misery expend their powers in the fields under the harsh sun in order to feed the mouths of the powerful and to fill the bellies of the tyrant? Do the people possess joy when the wretched look with defeated eyes at death the way the vanquished looks on a savior?

"What is peace, sweet Jesus? Is it in the eyes of children leaning on the breasts of hungry mothers in darkened, freezing huts? Or is it in needy bodies sleeping on stone beds, wishing for the slop that the priests of the monastery throw to their fattened pigs, but which they cannot have? What is joy, beautiful Jesus? Is it for a prince to buy with spare silver the abilities of men and the honor of women, and for us to be silent and remain slaves in spirit and in the flesh to those who dazzle our eyes with the shimmer of their golden medallions or the gleam of their gems and satiny robes? Or is it for us to cry out, recognizing our oppression and making our plaint, such that they send their hired men to attack us with swords, on fleet steeds, trampling the bodies of our women and little children and getting the earth drunk with our blood?

"Reach out your hand, Jesus the Powerful, and have mercy, for the hand of the despot is strong upon us. Or send death to lead us to graves where we can sleep peacefully, sheltered in the shadow of your cross until the day of your second coming. For life is no life as far as we are concerned, but a jet-black night in which evil phantoms strive to out-do one another, or a ravine crawling with horrifying snakes. Days are not days for us, but keen sword blades that the night hides in the covers on our beds and the morning unsheathes above our heads when our love of survival drags us to the fields. Show compassion, Jesus, on these masses gathered in your name on the day of your resurrection from the dead, and have mercy on their degradation and frailty."

Yuhanna stood there conversing confidentially with the heavens, while the crowd around him ran the gamut from pleased appreciation to angry condemnation.

One shouted, "He only spoke the truth, and he's talking about us before heaven because we are oppressed."

The one next to him said, "He is possessed, speaking with the tongue of an evil spirit."

"We never heard anything like this raving from our fathers and grandfathers, and we don't want to hear it now!"

Yet another whispered into the ear of his friend, "I felt a magical tremor jolt my heart when I heard his voice. He is speaking with a strange power."

His friend replied, "Yes, but our leaders know best what our needs are, and it is an error to doubt them."

The voices ascended from every side, gathering like the surging of a wave, and then they dissipated in the air. Meanwhile, one of the priests came and seized Yuhanna, surrendering him to the police, who took him to the mansion of the governor. When they tried to interrogate him, he said not a word in reply, remembering that Jesus had remained silent before his persecutors. They took him down into an unlit dungeon, where he slept in peace, propped against a stone wall.

The next morning, Yuhanna's father came and bore witness before the governor to the lunacy of his only child, saying, "How many times I have heard him ranting by himself, my lord, speaking about strange things with no truth to them. How many are the nights that he stayed up, talking to the silence with unknown words, calling out to imaginary beings in the dark with frightening sounds like the incantations of magicians and diviners. Ask the youth of the quarter, my lord, for they have sat with him and know that his reason is attracted to some distant world. They used to address him, but he would not reply, and should he speak, his words were ambiguous and unrelated to what they had said. Ask his mother, for she of all people knows best how his soul has been stripped of sense perception. She has seen him time and again gazing toward the horizon with a glassy-eyed, frozen stare, and heard him speaking passionately of trees, streams, flowers, and stars, just as infants speak about little things. Ask the monks of the monastery, for only yesterday he quarreled with them, scorning their devotions and worship, blaspheming against the holiness of their life.

"He is mad, my lord. But he is affectionate to me and to his mother, providing for us in our old age and expending the sweat of his brow so as to fulfill our needs. Have compassion on him in your compassion for us, and overlook his madness out of your respect for our parental love."

They released Yuhanna, and his insanity became notorious in those parts, so that youths mocked his words when they spoke of him and young girls looked at him with pitying eyes, saying, "Heaven has a strange way with human beings, for it gave this young man both a handsome face and a disturbed mind." They compared the gentle rays of his eyes with the darkness of his ailing soul.

∾

Among those meadows and knolls adorned with grasses and flowers, Yuhanna sat near his grazing calves, who had escaped the toils of humans through this fine pasture. Tears welled up in his eyes as he looked out at the villages and farms scattered over the slopes of the valley. He repeated these words over and over, with deep sighs: "You are many, and I am alone, so say what you like about me and do whatever you want with me. For the wolves devour the ewe in the dark of night, but the stains of her blood remain on the pebbles of the valley till the dawn arrives and the sun rises."